THE SQUIGGLE

by Carole Lexa Schaefer

illustrated by Pierr Morgan

Crown Publishers, Inc., New York

My teacher says, "Time to walk to the park." So, as always, off we go in a bunched-up, slow, tight, straight line.

I am last.
No one else sees what
I see on the sidewalk.

I grab it.

Slither slish.
It could be . . .

the dance of a big
scaly dragon.
Or . . .

Push-a-pat—
the top of a long
great wall.

Snap, tah-dah.
Maybe it's the path
of a circus acrobat.
Or . . .

Crack crickle hiss—
the sky trail of
popping fireworks.

Tug KA-BOOM!
It might be the
poof of a stormy
thundercloud.
Or . . .

Ripple
shhh—
the circle of
a deep still
pool.
Or even . . .

Ah-whoosh.
The rise of the full
fat moon.

Not so far ahead I see
my teacher and my class
shuffling along.
"Wait!" I call. "Look!"

Everyone turns around.

I show the
dragon,

the wall,

the acrobat,

the fireworks,

the storm
cloud,

the pool,

and the moon.

Everyone is smiling.

"Hoorayee!"
they cheer,
and grab on, too.
Then, off we go
to the park in our
slither slish,
push-a-pat,
snap, tah-dah,
crack crickle hiss,
tug KA-BOOM!
ripple shhh,
ah-whoosh

squiggle of a line.

To Judy, Mary, and Dave, who inspired my childhood play. And to Pierr, whose playful lines inspired this story.
—C. L. S.

To my teacher Agnes Haaga, a squiggler of all squigglers.
—P. M.

The art was done with Berol Prismacolor markers and Winsor and Newton gouache on 80-lb., 100%-recycled "Oatmeal" Speckle-tone paper from France.

Text copyright © 1996 by Carole Lexa Schaefer.
Illustrations copyright © 1996 by Pierr Morgan.

Published by Crown Publishers, Inc., a Random House company, 201 East 50th Street, New York, NY 10022

CROWN is a trademark of Crown Publishers, Inc.

Manufactured in Singapore.

Library of Congress Cataloging-in-Publication Data
Schaefer, Carole Lexa
The squiggle / by Carole Lexa Schaefer ; illustrated by Pierr Morgan. — 1st ed.
p.   cm.
Summary: As she walks to the park with her school class, a young girl finds a piece of string which her imagination turns into a dragon's tail, an acrobat, fireworks, a storm cloud, and more.
[1. Imagination—Fiction. 2. String—Fiction.] I. Morgan, Pierr, ill. II. Title.
PZ7.S3315Sq   1996   [E]—dc20   95-2299

ISBN 0-517-70047-6 (trade) 0-517-70048-4 (lib. bdg.)

10 9 8 7 6 5 4 3 2 1

First Edition

http://www.randomhouse.com/